MOONGOBBLE AND ME
THE NAUGHTY NORK

Books by Bruce Coville

Rod Allbright and the Galactic Patrol
Aliens Ate My Homework
I Left My Sneakers in Dimension X
The Search for Snout
Aliens Stole My Body

Moongobble and Me
The Dragon of Doom
The Weeping Werewolf
The Evil Elves
The Mischief Monster

My Teacher Books
My Teacher Is an Alien
My Teacher Fried My Brains
My Teacher Glows in the Dark
My Teacher Flunked the Planet

The Dragonslayers

Goblins in the Castle

I Was a Sixth Grade Alien

Available from Simon & Schuster

MOONGOBBLE AND ME
THE NAUGHTY NORK

Bruce Coville
illustrated by Katherine Coville

Simon & Schuster Books for Young Readers
New York London Toronto Sydney

For David and Lisa

SIMON & SCHUSTER BOOKS FOR YOUNG READERS
An imprint of Simon & Schuster Children's Publishing Division
1230 Avenue of the Americas, New York, New York 10020
Text copyright © 2008 by Bruce Coville
Illustrations copyright © 2008 by Katherine Coville
SIMON & SCHUSTER BOOKS FOR YOUNG READERS is a trademark of Simon & Schuster, Inc.
Book design by Tom Daly
The text for this book is set in Historical Fell Type.
The illustrations for this book are rendered in graphite.
Manufactured in the United States of America
2 4 6 8 10 9 7 5 3 1
Library of Congress Cataloging-in-Publication Data
Coville, Bruce.
The naughty Nork / Bruce Coville ; illustrated by Katherine Coville.
p. cm.—[Moongobble and me ; 5]
Summary: Edward, Fireball, Moongobble the magician and his faithful
toad, Urk, travel to Flitwick City, the Forest of Night, and Bogfester
Swamp on their quest to break the curse that turned their new friend,
Oggledy Nork, into a monster.
ISBN-13: 978-1-4169-0809-8 [hardcover]
ISBN-10: 1-4169-0809-9 [hardcover]
[1. Fairy tales. 2. Magicians—Fiction. 3. Blessing and
cursing—Fiction. 4. Monsters—Fiction.] I. Coville, Katherine, ill.
II. Title.
PZ8.C837Nau 2008
[Fic]—dc22   2008032417

FIRST EDITION

CONTENTS

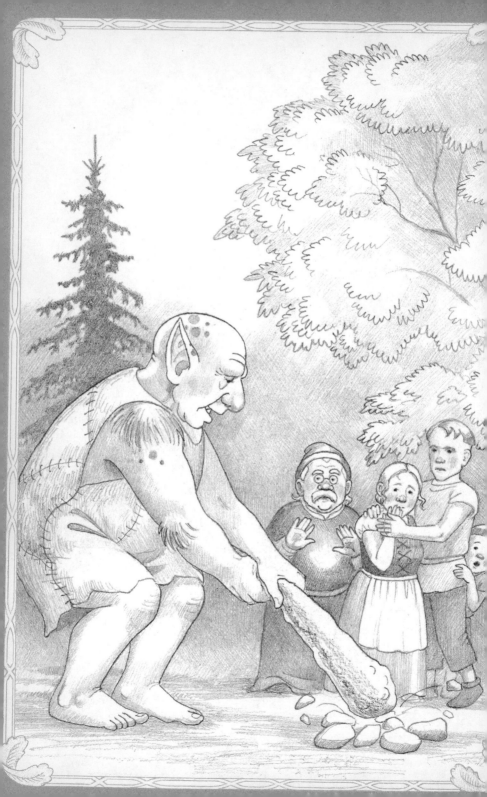

CHAPTER 1

A STRANGE GUEST

My mother was not entirely happy when I brought home a monster and asked if he could stay with us.

"Oh, Edward!" she said, rolling her eyes. "It's bad enough having you go off to strange places with Moongobble all the time. Your father and I certainly don't need you bringing strange people *back* with you!"

"But it's only for a little while! Just until we can fix him."

"Fix me!" growled Oggledy Nork happily.

Oggledy Nork was the monster we were talking

about. He was really very sweet, but I had to admit that there was a lot of him. He was almost twice as tall as my father, and his arms and legs bulged with muscles. He had no hair on his head, but his shoulders and elbows were pretty shaggy.

Also, he tended to drool a lot.

Moongobble stepped forward. Urk the toad was sitting on his shoulder.

Moongobble is a magician. He's also my boss, since I became his helper when he moved into the cottage on the hill. Moongobble is taller than me, but shorter than Father. He has a kind face, a shaggy white mustache, and a bit of a belly. He also has some mice living in his hat, which Mother thinks is disgusting.

Nothing much happened in Pigbone-East-of-the-Mountains before Moongobble came to live here. Life has been a lot more interesting since he arrived. Now I want things to stay just as they are.

"I would be glad to have Oggledy Nork stay at my house," said Moongobble. "But with all the magical items I have ... well, I'm afraid something bad might happen."

"Something bad," agreed Oggledy Nork, putting his finger on his lower lip and nodding his head wisely. Then he smiled as if he had just had a good idea. Picking up his club, he bellowed, "Oggledy Nork BASH bad things!" He looked around for a moment, then cried, "Like BUGS!"

He raised his club over his head, then crashed it down on a nearby rock, where a bug had been resting. The bug flew away. So did Fireball, the little dragon who is our friend. He had been sitting about three feet from the rock. But when Oggledy Nork's club came crashing down he darted into the air, spurting out a burst of flame.

As for the rock, it shattered into dozens of little pieces.

"Goodness!" cried Mother, looking alarmed.

Father stepped in front of her, as if to protect her.

"Oggledy Nork!" I said sharply. "No bashing!"

Oggledy Nork's lower lip trembled. He looked as if he was going to cry.

"No bashing?" he asked sadly.

"No bashing," I repeated firmly.

Oggledy Nork turned to Moongobble. "No bashing?"

Moongobble shook his head. "No bashing."

Oggledy Nork sighed, and his shoulders slumped. "No bashing?" he asked again, as if he was trying to understand the idea.

"Absolutely no bashing!" shouted Urk.

Oggledy Nork nodded, then roared happily, "Oggledy Nork understand! No bashing!"

"See?" I said. "He's really very nice."

"Nice!" said Oggledy Nork, smiling again.

The strange thing about Oggledy Nork was that he wasn't really a monster at all, at least not inside.

Inside, he was the brother of our friend the Rusty Knight.

It's just that he was under a curse.

We were planning to go on a quest to break that curse. I still had to convince my parents it was a good idea, but I was saving that problem for

later. Right now I just wanted them to let Oggledy Nork stay at our cottage.

"I will be glad to pay for his meals," offered Moongobble.

"Oh, goodness, it's not *that*," said my mother, though I knew feeding one more person really would be a problem. "It's just that . . . well . . ."

She turned to my father, as if she wasn't sure what to say.

Father cleared his throat. "It's just that I'd rather not have things upset your mother right now, Edward."

"I never want to upset Mother. But why is now any worse than any other time?"

Father slipped an arm around her shoulder and said softly, "Because she's going to have a baby."

"Baby!" roared Oggledy Nork happily. "Me like babies!"

I didn't say anything.

I was too shocked to speak.

CHAPTER 2

PLANNING

We finally decided to take Oggledy Nork to the Rusty Knight's cottage. Since they were brothers, it seemed like the best place for him to stay. On the other hand, it meant I would have to stay with him, so he wouldn't get in trouble.

"Whoo," said Urk, when we went inside. "We should change his name to the *Dusty* Knight. This place is even messier than *your* house, Moongobble!"

"House need cleaning!" roared Oggledy Nork, who had had to drop to his hands and knees to get through the door. "Me clean it good!"

To our amazement, he started to do just *that*. In fact, he actually seemed to like sweeping and dusting.

Later that afternoon, we were sitting at the Rusty Knight's table. Well, Moongobble and I were at the table. Urk was sitting *on* the table. And Fireball was perched on my shoulder. The chairs were too small for Oggledy Nork, of course. He was sitting in the corner, pulling the petals off some daisies he had picked after he finished sweeping.

"He'd be handy to have around, if he weren't so dang big," said Urk, glancing at the monster.

I didn't answer.

"What's the matter, Edward?" asked Fireball. "You seem worried."

I didn't want to answer him, but finally I couldn't keep it inside anymore. "I can't believe my mother is going to have a baby!" I blurted.

"Oh, cheer up," said Urk. "At least *your* mother only has them one at a time. When I was a tadpole I had about a thousand brothers and sisters."

"What happened to them?" I asked.

Urk shrugged his warty shoulders. "I lost track after I left the swamp."

"Why did you leave?"

"You know I don't like to talk about my past, Edward. Let's get down to business!"

By "business," he meant the problem of figuring out what to do about Oggledy Nork. We had left his brother, the Rusty Knight, back at Fortress Nork. That was another part of the curse: One brother always had to stay at the old family home. But I had a question about that. "There's something I don't understand," I said.

"What is it?" asked Moongobble.

"Well, I thought the brother who stayed at the family home was supposed to turn into Oggledy Nork. So why is *this* brother still the Oggledy? Shouldn't he be turning back now?"

Moongobble tapped on his nose, a sign that he was thinking. "I'm a little confused about that myself. I think maybe this brother has been Oggledy Nork for so long that the spell has gotten stuck."

All we knew about the spell was that it had been

cast by an old woman who had been offended by one of the Rusty Knight's ancestors.

"The first problem in removing the curse is that we won't be able to find the woman who cast the spell," continued Moongobble.

"Why not?" I asked.

"It happened more than a hundred years ago. She'll be dead by now!"

I felt silly, until Urk said, "I wouldn't be too sure of that, Moongobble. Some of those old ladies who know magic can stick around for a long time. A *long* time."

"I have an idea!" cried Moongobble, snapping his fingers.

A puff of green smoke rose from the tips of his fingers.

He stared at the smoke in surprise. "Oh, dear! I hope I didn't turn anything into cheese!"

We all looked around. Nothing seemed to have been cheese-ified.

"Well, that's a relief," grumbled

Urk. "I keep telling you that you have to be careful now that your magic is starting to improve. A careless snap like that could cause a real problem someday."

I didn't blame Urk for being nervous. Not long ago Moongobble had turned him into a little pink cat.

"I'll be more careful," promised Moongobble. He linked his hands in front of himself, so he couldn't accidentally cast a spell. "There, feel safer now?"

"Not really," said Urk, rolling his big eyes. "Just tell us your idea!"

"Well, do you remember that Fazwad invited me to Flitwick City for the next meeting of the Society of Magicians?"

Fazwad is head of the Society of Magicians. He used to be a problem for Moongobble, but he's our friend now. At least, I think he is. I haven't decided whether I completely trust him yet.

"I remember," said Urk. "What about it?"

"I can go ask for advice there!"

Urk blinked. "That's not a bad idea. They probably have records we can search too."

I loved that word, *we*. "Does that mean we're *all* going?" I cried.

"Of course," said Moongobble. "You are my helper, aren't you?"

I smiled. "I've always wanted to go to Flitwick City!"

Urk snorted. "That's because you've never been there. Cities. Feh. They're all noise and people and horses and horse poop. I hate cities!"

"You don't have to come if you don't want to," said Moongobble gently.

"Of course I'll come! You think I'd let you go alone? Who knows what kind of trouble you'd get in without me?"

"Thank you," said Moongobble.

"Don't mention it," grumbled Urk. "Ever. Besides, we've still got one very big problem to solve."

"What problem is that?" I asked.

Just then we heard a crashing sound.

"Uh-oh," said Oggledy Nork.

"Him," said Urk. "What are we going to do about him?"

CHAPTER 3

SEEMING

We all turned toward Oggledy Nork.

"Broken," he said sadly, pointing to the shattered pieces of a vase he had been trying to cram his daisies into. "Oggledy Nork brokened it!"

"See what I mean?" said Urk. "The big problem—and I do mean *big*—is: What are we going to do about him? We can't just leave him here."

Urk was right about that. I shuddered to think of the trouble our monstrous friend might cause if we left him in Pigbone.

"Well, we'll just have to take him with us," said Moongobble.

"That would seem like the best idea," said Urk. "Except for one thing: They don't like monsters in Flitwick City. In fact, I think they have a law against them."

"He will be awfully noticeable," admitted Moongobble.

"Noticeable?" yelped Urk. "He'll terrify any sensible person!"

Looking up from the broken vase, Oggledy Nork said, "Me not terrifying. Me nice!"

"You're very nice," replied Moongobble.

Oggledy Nork drooled happily. Then he pushed aside the pieces of the vase and started pulling the petals off one of the daisies, chanting, "Me love me, me love me not. Oh, me *love* me! YAAAAY!"

"Maybe we could disguise him," I said.

"As what?" asked Fireball. "A talking tree?"

"I know!" cried Moongobble. "I'll cast a spell of seeming on him."

I wrinkled my brow. "What's a 'spell of seeming'?"

"It makes one thing *seem* like another. I was reading about them just last night."

I glanced at Urk. He looked as nervous as I felt.

Moongobble is very, very nice. But his magic doesn't always work quite the way it should.

Ten minutes later we had a kitchen chair that *seemed* like a bathtub, a stack of books that *seemed* like a pine tree, and a broom that *seemed* like a slender young lady.

Oggledy Nork, on the other hand, still seemed like nothing but himself.

"I don't understand," said Moongobble, shaking

his wand. "Usually if a spell doesn't work, it would at least change him into cheese!"

"Maybe it's a side effect of the curse," said Urk. "Other magic bounces off him."

"I'll try again," said Moongobble, giving his wand another shake. "This time I'll make the magic visible."

"For heaven's sake, quit while you're ahead!" bellowed Urk.

He was too late. Moongobble cast one more spell. A ray of green light shot out of the end of his wand. It bounced off Oggledy Nork, hit the mirror, careened off two walls, then blasted straight into me.

Magic prickled over my skin. I didn't actually feel myself stretch or grow or change in any way. But when I looked at my hands, they *seemed* to be much bigger.

I hurried to the mirror. I *seemed* to be a tall, handsome knight!

"You and the broom would make a nice couple," said Urk.

I looked at the broom nervously. Fortunately, even though it *seemed* like a beautiful young woman, it was really still just a broomstick.

Urk turned to Moongobble and said, "Why don't you change everything back? We'll have to disguise Oggledy Nork some other way."

Moongobble sighed and started trying to reverse the spells. It took almost an hour, and I seemed like a blacksmith, a priest, a goat, a bear, a woodchuck, and an old lady before he was done.

I had liked looking like a tall, handsome knight. Even so, it was a relief to just look like myself again.

"Cheer up, Edward," muttered Urk. "At least he didn't turn you into cheese."

"That's true," I said. I had already been cheese once, and that was enough. "But we still have to figure out how to get Oggledy Nork into the city."

We sat for several minutes, thinking. Suddenly Urk cried, "I know! We'll dress him up as a woman. People are much nicer to women than they are to monsters. We can put him in a dress and wrap a scarf over his head. If he crouches down a little he'll just seem like a big—well, *very* big—and fairly ugly woman."

"Ugly!" said Oggledy Nork happily.

We had to get my mother to help with this part.

The nice thing was, by the time we were done dressing Oggledy Nork, she had decided he wasn't so bad after all.

"He's really very sweet," she whispered to me. "If only he wasn't so big!"

Moongobble was giving Oggledy Nork some instructions. "Now, for heaven's sake, be quiet," he warned. "If anyone hears you talk, they'll know you're not a woman."

"Quiet!" bellowed Oggledy Nork, plucking at his dress. "Me VERY quiet."

"Good grief," muttered Urk. "You might as well tell him to be little, Moongobble!"

"Little!" said Oggledy Nork happily, crouching down so he was only a few feet taller than me. "Me VERY little."

"Stay right there," ordered Mother. Stepping over to him, she draped a tablecloth over his head, then tied it under his chin. She had stitched some yellow yarn on the front of it, to make it look like he had hair. She stood back to study her work, then muttered, "Well, I don't know if anyone will believe it, but that's about as good as it's going to get."

"Then we should be on our way," said Moongobble.

Father shook my hand. Mother kissed me on the forehead and said, "Behave yourself, Edward." Turning to Oggledy Nork, she added, "You be good, too."

"GOOD!" bellowed Oggledy Nork, nodding in agreement. "Good, quiet, *little* Oggledy Nork!"

And with that, we started for Flitwick City.

CHAPTER 4

SNORING

Unless you take a shortcut through the Forest of Night, it's a two-day walk from Pigbone to Flitwick City. We weren't really afraid of the forest—we had gone there when we went to fetch tears from the Weeping Werewolf for Moongobble's second Mighty Task. Even so, the Forest of Night is the kind of place you only enter if you really have to.

So we took the path around it.

As the sun began to set, Urk said, "We'd better look for a place to camp."

"I'll go," said Fireball. He was very handy for this

kind of thing, because he could fly a hundred feet up and scout out a lot of places very quickly. In fact, it was only about ten minutes before he came fluttering back, saying, "I spotted a good place. It's a little way ahead, then just off to the right. Follow me."

Soon we were standing in an open space that had a little stream running along one edge of it.

"You're right, Fireball," said Urk. "This is a very nice spot to camp."

I figured if Urk bothered to say it was nice, it must be very nice indeed!

Nice or not, I didn't get much sleep that night. That was because Oggledy Nork started to snore. Well, he didn't just snore. I'd heard snores ever since we broke the curse of the Weeping Werewolf and I brought my Father back home. But the noise coming from Oggledy Nork was like nothing I had ever heard before.

"At least we won't have to worry about bears," muttered Urk, who was crouched near my ear. "Or monsters, for that matter. Those snores will frighten away anything that comes near us!"

Grumbling to himself, he pulled his little blanket over his head.

I doubt it did him much good.

After a few hours, Moongobble said, "I've got to do something about this! We have to be rested when we visit the Society of Magicians."

Urk poked his head from under his blanket. "What do you have in mind?"

"Just watch!" replied Moongobble. Getting to his feet, he raised his wand and chanted, "Iggledy, Biggledy, We Need Quiet, Silence Those Snores and Stop This Riot!"

A sound like little bells filled the clearing.

A shimmering blue bubble formed over Oggledy Nork.

The bells stopped, followed by a perfect silence.

"It worked!" cried Moongobble. He sounded a bit surprised.

"What is that thing?" asked Urk.

"A Bubble of Silence," said Moongobble proudly.

Urk hopped to the Bubble of Silence and poked at it. His toadly finger dented the blue surface, but didn't go through. "Nicely done, Moongobble," he said. But once he had hopped back to me, he muttered, "I'm not so sure about that bubble."

"Why not?" I asked.

"I don't know. I just have a feeling that something might go wrong with it."

I wanted to ask more, but he pulled his blanket over his head again. After a minute, he began to snore himself. Fortunately, it was much quieter than Oggledy Nork—more like a mouse farting.

In the middle of the night I was woken by a squeaking sound.

I opened my eyes. The sky was spangled with stars. A cool breeze rustled through my hair. The smell of the forest was all around me. It was so beautiful that I forgot for a second what had woken me.

Then I heard the squeaking again.

It came from the direction of Oggledy Nork.

I got to my knees and turned to look.

Moongobble's Bubble of Silence was still in place. But it had gotten bigger—*much* bigger.

It had been a pretty blue when Moongobble first made it.

Now it was a dark, swampy green.

It had the look of magic gone bad.

Then I saw something else, something that filled me with fear.

Someone was about to poke the bubble.

"Don't!" I cried.

I was too late.

The person poked.

The bubble burst.

CHAPTER 5

FLITWICK CITY

Actually, the bubble didn't just burst.

It exploded.

I flung myself down and covered my head. Every snore that had been trapped inside the bubble since Moongobble cast his spell came rushing out. Even with my hands over my ears it sounded like fourteen bears having a fight during a thunderstorm.

I'm not even going to try to describe the smell.

Moongobble jumped to his feet, blinking in surprise.

Fireball screeched and flew straight into the air, shooting out a burst of flame.

Urk bellowed, "It's the end of the world!" Still clutching his little blanket, he hopped under a nearby bush.

Oggledy Nork didn't even wake up.

When the only sound left was the Oggledy Nork's *new* snores, Urk crept out from under the bush. "I knew that bubble was a bad idea," he grumbled.

"I thought it was exciting!" said a little voice. It came from where Oggledy Nork was snoring, but it was clearly not his voice.

Even so, we all knew who it belonged to.

Raising his wand, Moongobble chanted, "Iggle,

Biggle, Ternon Daglo!" His hat made a fizzing sound, then began to shine.

It was kind of a silly way to get light, but it was the best spell he had so far.

By the hat's light we saw a foot-high, pointy-eared little monster standing next to Oggledy Nork. She wore a dress made of pink flower petals and was looking very pleased with herself.

"Snelly!" cried Urk in horror.

"Hi, Urkie! C'mere. I wanna hug you!"

Urk jumped in my direction, in case he needed me to shield him.

"Snelly, what are *you* doing here?" demanded Moongobble.

"I came to help!"

Since Snelly is a Mischief Monster and her hobby is causing trouble, it was hard to imagine her actually helping with anything.

Moongobble looked at her sternly. "Does your mother know you're here?"

This was an important question. Snelly's mother is queen of the Mischief Monsters, and someone you definitely don't want mad at you.

"Yep! Momma said I could come. She said we owe the Rusty Knight and Oggledy Nork a favor for taking care of my stinky-pie little brother while he was still an egg." She sighed, then added, "She also said I was getting on her nerves."

That was easy to believe. Snelly was the most annoying creature I had ever met.

Suddenly Oggledy Nork stopped snoring. "Snelly?" he asked, sitting up.

"Hi, Oggy!" she cried happily. "I came to help!" She jumped into his lap, then climbed onto his shoulder. "Why are you wearing this scarf?"

"He's in disguise," I explained. "We thought people might be less afraid of him that way."

Snelly laughed. "Good idea! It's like mischief!" She turned to Moongobble. "I'm sorry I popped your big green bubble. But it sure was exciting when all that sound came out!"

"It's probably just as well," said Moongobble with a sigh. "Who knows what might have happened if it had burst on its own?"

Morning light was beginning to filter through the trees.

"We might as well eat some breakfast and get going," grumbled Urk.

We moved more slowly now, since we had to stop every ten minutes or so to keep Snelly from grabbing Urk. Just before noon we reached the top of a hill. Looking into the valley below, I cried, "What's *that*?"

Urk chuckled. "*That*, Edward, is Flitwick City."

"But it's so . . . so *big*!"

You have to remember, I have lived in Pigbone all my life. We only have fifteen cottages in the whole town. Flitwick City had houses that were bigger than all fifteen cottages put together. It also had towers, and castles, and things I didn't even know the names for.

The whole city was surrounded by a high wall. From where we stood, I could see that the wall had four gates. A road led to each gate, and each road was crowded with travelers—some walking, some on horseback, some in carts.

"It looks scary," I said.

Urk laughed. "Edward, you've been through the Forest of Night. You've come face to face with a dragon, and a werewolf—"

"And my mother!" put in Snelly with a shudder.

"And Snelly's mother," agreed Urk. "Why would this frighten you?"

"I don't know. It's just that there are so many . . . people."

"People," said Oggledy Nork, nodding in agreement. "People scary!"

"Scary or not, we're going in," said Moongobble. "Let's get moving!"

"Not yet," said Urk. "I told you, they don't allow

monsters. We have to do something about Snelly. Fireball, too, probably."

It took a while, but finally we stuffed Snelly inside the front of Oggledy Nork's dress. He was so big, and she was so small, that it hardly made a difference once we had her strapped in. Fireball curled himself up—he was a lot longer than he was thick— and we managed to tuck him into my pack. Which left Oggledy Nork.

"Now, for heaven's sake, be quiet," ordered Moongobble.

"QUIET!" agreed Oggledy Nork, at the top of his lungs.

"And remember to crouch down so you don't look so big."

"LITTLE!" bellowed Oggledy Nork.

Urk sighed and said, "This isn't going to be easy."

With that, we started down the hill toward Flitwick City.

CHAPTER 6

THE HALL OF MAGIC

At the gate we were stopped by two guards dressed in fancy outfits. A big sign on the wall beside them said NO MONSTERS ALLOWED IN CITY.

"Crouch down a little more," I whispered to Oggledy Nork, glad that we had disguised him.

"What is your business in Flitwick City?" asked the tallest guard.

Standing up straight, Moongobble said, "I am Moongobble the Magician. I have come to attend a meeting of the Society of Magicians."

"What about the boy?" asked the other guard.

"He is my assistant."

"And the toad?"

"Another assistant."

"And the old lady?"

Moongobble paused, then said firmly, "She's my mother."

The tone of his voice made it clear he didn't want to hear any rude comments about how big and ugly his mother was.

The first guard shrugged. "We'd better let 'em in, Harry. You know how Fazwad gets if we stop any of his friends."

"All right, all right," said the second guard. "Go on in. But don't let us hear about you causing any trouble!"

We passed through the gate into the city. "I didn't know there were this many people in the world!" I said softly. Then I wrinkled my nose. "And what's that smell?"

"Horse poop," muttered Urk. "Lots and lots of horse poop."

A squishy feeling beneath my foot let me know that he was right.

We could have made a dozen trips from one end of Pigbone to the other in the time it took us to reach the Hall of Magic. When we finally did get there, I was disappointed. Despite how grand the city was, the Hall of Magic was surprisingly plain, and hardly bigger than our cottage.

Moongobble knocked on the door.

"Hey!" it shouted, opening a pair of large blue eyes. "Watch it, buster!"

Moongobble jumped back in surprise.

"State your business," ordered the door. "And keep your hands to yourself! You almost gave me a black eye."

Moongobble cleared his throat, then made a little bow. "I am Moongobble the Magician. I am here for today's meeting."

The door narrowed its eyes. "Let me check my records," it said suspiciously. Then the eyes disappeared altogether.

"Snooty dang door," muttered Urk.

"I heard that!" snapped the door. Several minutes went by, and I wondered if the door was making us wait, just to be mean. Finally it growled, "All right, you're cleared for admission. However, only Moongobble is allowed past the Waiting Room."

Then it creaked open.

The space beyond was pitch black.

"Scary," murmured Oggledy Nork.

"Well, we're going in anyway," said Moongobble. He took a deep breath, then marched right into the blackness. A brief sparkle of light surrounded him, then he disappeared.

Urk, who was sitting on my shoulder, said, "We'd better follow him, Edward, before he gets himself in trouble."

Snelly stuck her head out of Oggledy Nork's dress and said, "Stay close behind, Oggy. We don't want to lose them."

"Oggledy Nork stay very close," he agreed.

I stepped through the door. Strange tingles skittered over my skin. For a second I felt sick to my stomach. Then I was inside the Hall of Magic.

I gasped in surprise. The room we now stood in could have held five of my cottages and still not felt crowded.

And this was just the Waiting Room!

Several magicians were wandering around. I recognized some of them from the party we had held after Moongobble finished his third Mighty Task. Two or three of them called out to us. A moment later Fazwad appeared—without his usual puff of blue smoke, I noticed.

"Greetings, Moongobble!" he said, walking toward us. "I'm glad you could make it!" He stopped and frowned a little. "But I didn't expect you to bring so many . . . others with you."

Moongobble quickly explained what had happened since Fazwad's last visit to the cottage.

"Ah, an old family curse," said Fazwad, glancing at Oggledy Nork, who made a charming curtsey in response. "Very interesting. Well, the meeting is about to start. Come on in. And bring—what was his name again?"

"Oggledy Nork," said Moongobble.

"Yes. Bring Oggledy Nork with you. Edward, you and the others will have to stay here in the Waiting Room. Please don't touch anything. It could be dangerous."

"Thank you for the warning," I said.

"It was as much for my sake as yours. I don't want to have to clean up after any explosions, much less have to try to put you back together again. Come along, Moongobble. You, too, Oggledy Nork."

I had noticed other magicians going through a big door at the back of the room. Now Moongobble, Fazwad, and Oggledy Nork passed through it as well. A moment later the door swung shut behind them.

"I still don't like that guy," grumbled Urk.

"But I like this room," said Fireball, climbing

out of my pack and fluttering upward. "It has lots of space to fly in!" He began to flap in big circles around the ceiling.

"What's this?" asked Snelly.

She was standing next to a table, holding a small blue bottle.

"I don't know and I don't care," snapped Urk. "You heard what Fazwad said. Leave things alone!"

"Don't be a stinky-pie, Urk. Come here. I wanna hug you!"

"You just stay right where you are!" bellowed Urk as he scrambled from my shoulder to my head. "Don't move too fast, Edward," he muttered as he climbed past my ear. "I don't want to slip and fall!"

I noticed a pair of mirrors on the wall. Wondering why there were two of them, I went to have a look. In the first mirror I saw Urk and myself, and the room behind me. But the second mirror wasn't a mirror at all. It wasn't a window, either—at least not a normal one, since it didn't look out on the city. What it showed instead was a wide beach with big waves crashing against the sand.

"What is this?" I asked nervously.

"It's called the ocean," said Urk.

"No, I mean the thing we're looking into."

"It's a magic window. It shows scenes from all over the world."

The image shifted to a forest. A unicorn was walking through the woods. It reminded me of the one we had seen when we went to get the evil stone called the Queen's Belly Button. The picture changed again, this time showing a snow-covered mountain top.

I could have watched the magic window for a long time, but suddenly Urk yelled, "Snelly, *don't*!"

I turned so fast Urk nearly slid off my head.

Snelly was holding a wooden box.

And she was about to lift the lid.

CHAPTER 7

THE BEAUTIFUL LADY

"Put the box down, Snelly!" said Urk.

"Why? It says *Open me for a beautiful experience*! I think you're *supposed* to open it!"

Before I could take a step toward her, she opened it.

A burst of purple smoke swirled out, wrapping itself around Snelly. Soon I couldn't see her at all, though I could hear her coughing.

"Fireball!" I called. "Flap away the smoke!"

The little dragon fluttered down and began to circle the purple cloud. The haze drifted away.

Snelly was gone. In her place stood a tall, beautiful woman with long golden hair. Her dress was made of flower petals, just like Snelly's, but her shape was very different. The woman looked at her hands. Her eyes widened. She grabbed some of the yellow hair flowing over her shoulder and looked at it in horror.

"What the heck happened to me?"

The voice made it clear: Despite the way she looked, the beautiful woman was Snelly!

She ran to the non-magic mirror, stared at it in disgust, then whined, "I can't look like this!"

"Why not?" I asked. "You're beautiful!"

"I'm a monster! I don't wanna be beautiful!"

"Well, the box did say it would give you a beautiful experience," said Urk sweetly.

"It didn't

say it would do *this*!" shrieked Snelly. "They shouldn't leave something like that just lying around. Some kid might open it!"

"Some kid *did* open it," Urk pointed out. "But that kid was warned not to, wasn't she?"

Before Snelly could reply, the door opened. Moongobble and Fazwad stepped out, with Oggledy Nork stumping along behind them. When he saw the beautiful woman, Fazwad groaned. "Snelly, I told you not to touch anything!"

"You didn't expect me to pay attention, did you?" Given Snelly's personality, the question almost made sense. "Now turn me back!"

Fazwad spread his hands. "What makes you think I can do that? You'll have to let it wear off."

"How long will *that* take?"

Fazwad shrugged. "It differs from person to person. I expect it will take at least three or four years."

"YEARS?!" howled Snelly. She threw herself to the floor and began to kick and scream. "I don't wanna be a pretty lady! I wanna be myself!"

"You should have thought of that before you opened the box, dear," said Moongobble gently.

"But I can only deal with one spell at a time, and right now we have to work on Oggledy Nork's problem. According to Fazwad, the first thing we should do is visit Tambo and Timbo."

"Who are Tambo and Timbo?" I asked.

"They run the archives," said Fazwad.

"Ark hives?" Oggledy Nork shuddered. "Me no like bees!"

"Archives!" bellowed Urk. "It's a place where they keep lists of things that have happened."

"Exactly," said Moongobble. "The good news is, any curse ever cast will be recorded there. So with a little time we should be able to find out who cast the curse, and how to remove it."

"Where are these archives?" asked Urk.

"Right downstairs," said Fazwad. He started toward a wall. For a second I thought he was going to bump into it, but as he got closer a door appeared. It opened without him even touching it.

We followed Fazwad down a long winding stairway that was lit by floating balls of green and yellow light. One grazed my cheek as I went by. I flinched, afraid it would burn me, but it was cool against my skin.

At last we came to a big wooden door.

Fazwad cleared his throat. The door swung open.

We stepped into a large room.

I looked around in wonder. Scrolls and papers were scattered everywhere. Stacks of books rose from the floor, some of them twice as tall as me. Other stacks leaned against shelves that held yet more books. In front of those shelves were tables covered with more books, and about a dozen snoozing cats. Some of the books were open, some closed. Two actually had balls of light around them.

"Can I help you?"

I looked around. The words seemed to come from nowhere.

CHAPTER 8

TAMBO AND TIMBO

"Is this room magic?" I whispered.

A short, roundish woman raised her head from behind one of the tables. Glaring at me, she said, "No, the room's not magic! I was just getting a book."

"Ah, there you are, Tambo!" cried Fazwad. "We've come to find out about a curse."

"Curses are Timbo's department," said Tambo. Turning toward the rows of shelves that stretched behind her, she shouted, "TIMBO! Get out here! We have company."

"Coming!" called a voice from somewhere in the distance. "Coming!"

A minute later a tall, heavyset man ambled out from among the shelves. He had a black-and-white cat walking at his heels, a black cat in his arms, and a ginger-colored cat draped over his shoulder.

"Greetings!" he cried cheerfully. "What can we do for you?"

"We need to find out about a curse," said Moongobble.

"Excellent! I love curses."

"You do not," said Tambo. "They're awful things. You love studying them. That's different."

"What kind of curse is it?" asked Timbo, rolling on as if Tambo hadn't said anything.

"It *my* curse," said Oggledy Nork proudly.

Timbo blinked. "Goodness, you are a big . . . um, something, aren't you?"

"Big!" agreed Oggledy Nork happily. "Cursed, too!"

Tambo, who was looking at him carefully, said, "You know, Timbo, I think that's an Oggledy!"

"Really?" cried Timbo. "A genuine Oggledy?"

46

"What's an Oggledy?" asked Moongobble.

"ME!" roared Oggledy Nork proudly. "ME an Oggledy!"

"I guess I was right," said Tambo.

"But what *is* an Oggledy?" I asked.

"Ah," said Timbo. "Well, you see, an Oggledy is the result of a very specific kind of curse. They began about four hundred years ago with—"

"Timbo," said Tambo. Her voice had a warning note in it.

"—an old king named Oggle," continued Timbo, ignoring her interruption. "He was upset because—"

"Timbo," said Tambo again.

"—his daughter had decided to—"

"*Timbo . . .*"

"—run off with—"

"TIMBO! Just tell them what an Oggledy is. They don't need the whole history. It takes three days to tell it!"

Timbo blinked. "Oh. Well, the short version is that an Oggledy is something like an ogre, only a lot nicer."

"Nicer!" said Oggledy Nork happily.

"Er, yes," said Timbo, sounding slightly nervous. "Nicer. But what's really interesting is that it's a progressive curse, one tied to both place and family."

Tambo sighed.

"So once the Oggledy Curse has been placed on a family, it goes on and on, until it's finally broken."

"But *how* do you break it?" cried Urk. "That's what we want to know!"

"Oh," said Timbo. "Well, that depends on who cast it. Hmm. As far as I know, the only person who's been able to cast one of those spells for the last hundred years is the Old Woman who lives in the Forest of Night."

His words sent fear whispering down my spine.

CHAPTER 9

THE OLD WOMAN

"Not her again," groaned Urk.

I felt the way Urk sounded. We had met that old woman, and she was nasty, cranky, and scary. Even worse, she was the person who had turned my father into the Weeping Werewolf.

"Ah," said Fazwad, pulling on his lower lip. "I see. Well, it makes a certain amount of sense that it would be her."

"It does?" I said. "Why?"

"Probably because the old bat's been causing trouble for a few hundred years now," said Timbo.

"Timbo!" said Tambo.

"Well, she has," said Timbo stubbornly.

"How can she have lived so long?" I asked.

"Magic, of course," said Tambo. She shivered. "And not pretty magic, either."

We spent the night in the Hall of Magic. Though my bed was the most comfortable one I'd ever slept in, the way the sheets kept tucking themselves in around me all by themselves made me kind of nervous. Also, I wasn't sure I liked the way my pillow tried to sing me to sleep.

In the morning Fazwad took us to the kitchen. It was huge! But the food the cook gave us was just some tiny packages wrapped in paper. I looked at the ones in my hand. They were hardly bigger than acorns.

"What good will these do us?" I asked.

"You'll see," said the cook with a smile.

I sighed. Magicians like to keep things so mysterious!

The cook handed another packet to Snelly, saying, "This one's for the beautiful lady."

"I'm not beautiful! I'm a little monster!"

The cook blinked, and Fazwad hustled us out of the room.

The closer we got to the Forest of Night, the more nervous I felt. It didn't help that several animals stopped us along the way to say, "Do you know where you're going? Turn back now if you have any sense!"

"Thank you," said Moongobble politely each time this happened. "But we know what we're doing."

The last of these animals was a squirrel. When he heard Moongobble's answer, he shrugged and said, "You guys are such nuts, I should save you for the winter!"

He laughed at his own joke, then bounded into the brush.

An hour later we entered the Forest of Night.

You can tell when you enter the Forest of Night because the world instantly gets darker and gloomier. It's as if night and day are struggling for control, and night is winning.

When the blackness of *real* night—a deeper,

darker blackness—began closing in, we stopped to make camp.

"We might as well try this food," I said, taking out one of the little packets the cook had given us. I started to unwrap it. At once, a wonderful smell drifted to my nose. The paper began to unfold by itself. In a few seconds I was holding a big plate covered with hot roasted chicken, potatoes (with gravy!), and some blue-and-purple beans.

"Mmmmmmm!" said Oggledy Nork when we unwrapped a package for him.

I agreed.

The next morning we reached the old woman's cave. As before, Fireball talked our way past the hissing snakes that hung down over the entrance.

"I hate those things," muttered Urk, who was riding on my shoulder.

"Why?" I asked.

"Well, other than the fact that they eat toads, I suppose there's no real reason. Just call it a foolish whim!"

I didn't reply, because cold fear was starting to

grip my stomach. We were approaching the woman who had cursed my father.

She was also the woman who had cursed the Rusty Knight's family.

Who was she?

Why did she do these things?

As before, we found the old woman sitting in a chair at the back of the cave. She looked like a pile of wrinkles that had somehow managed to climb into a dress.

"Well, well, well," she creaked, when we were standing in front of her. "Look who's back!" She narrowed her eyes. "What do you want this time, *fools*?"

"We wish to lift the curse you placed on the Family Nork," said Moongobble.

For a second I thought the old woman looked surprised. But she quickly twisted her face into a scowl, and said, "That will take some doing. Are you prepared for a Mighty Task?"

"Again with the

Mighty Tasks," muttered Urk. "What is it with these people?"

"Silence, toad! You want a curse lifted, you perform a Mighty Task. It's that simple."

"What would that task be?" asked Moongobble, his voice small and humble.

The old woman smiled, which made me nervous. Then she said, "You must remove the curse that sits on *me*!"

CHAPTER 10

THE OLD WOMAN'S STORY

"*You* have a curse on you?" I cried.

"Don't we all?" replied the old woman.

"Well, that's gloomy," said Urk.

"Silence, toad!" she snapped again.

"Hey!" cried Snelly. "Don't you be mean to Urkie!"

The old woman looked at her, then said shrewdly, "That voice does not go with that body. In fact, you sound like a Mischief Monster to me. What in the world are you doing looking like that, girlie?"

"I'm cursed too," said Snelly sadly. "Cursed to be beautiful."

"Well, don't worry. It will wear off sooner or later. That kind of beauty always does."

"I would still like to know your story," said Moongobble.

I was amazed at the kindness in his voice. I think the old woman heard it too, because she looked at him carefully for quite a while, then sighed and said, "It began in Bogfester Swamp, long, long ago."

I shuddered. We had crossed Bogfester Swamp once. It was not a pleasant place.

Plucking at her dress, she said, "I was out gathering toads the night it started."

"Gathering toads?" I asked. I felt Urk shift on my shoulder.

"My grandmother used them for her spells. And if you interrupt me one more time, I may decide to show you what she did with them!"

I nodded, and bit my lips together. This was something I didn't want to find out.

The old woman stared at me fiercely for a moment, then continued her story.

"I was gathering toads, as I had so often, when the biggest toad I ever saw leaped out of the brush, landed on my shoulder, spit in my ear, and croaked, 'Let's see how you like it!'"

"Oh, geez," whispered Urk. Fortunately, he said it so softly the old woman didn't hear him. I wanted to talk to him, to ask what the matter was, but I didn't dare.

The old woman shuddered, as if remembering something awful, then said, "An instant later I was a toad."

"How did you turn back?" asked Moongobble.

"I didn't. At least not permanently. I had become a were-toad."

I gasped. "You mean . . ."

I clamped my hand over my mouth, terrified that she would do something terrible to me for interrupting. But she just sighed and said, "It's exactly as you think. I was doomed to become a toad every full moon.

"For two years I told no one of my curse. Then, one night when I was hopping through the swamp I heard a voice cry, 'Lady! Hey, lady! You are the most beautiful toad I have ever seen!'

"I stopped. Bounding toward me was a very

handsome he-toad. Well, he was handsome as toads go. I thought about fleeing—I hated being seen when I was a toad. But except for the big toad who had cursed me, this was the first toad who had ever spoken to me. He stopped in front of me and said, 'You understood me?'

"'Of course,' I replied.

"'You are not a normal toad, are you?' he asked.

"'No more than are you,' I answered."

The old woman paused and stared into the distance, lost in her memories. "That was how it began," she said at last. "We would meet once a month in the swamp. He called me his little toadlietta; I called him my warty prince. It turned out he was under a curse as well.

"After a while we fell in love. How could we not? After all, who else was there who could understand our secret?

"Except it turned out later that he had another secret as well. In his human life he was betrothed to a beautiful lady from a normal family."

She turned her head away, and in the low light I could have sworn I saw a tear trickle down her cheek.

"I never told him I found out. I simply swore I would get my revenge."

"And did you?" asked Snelly.

A wicked smile creased the old woman's wrinkled face. "Oh, of course I did, dearie. Why do you think that thing standing behind you is an Oggledy? He bears the curse I first placed on his ancestor, who betrayed me so long ago!"

I glanced behind me at Oggledy Nork, wondering what he thought about this.

Mostly he just looked confused.

Moongobble spoke up. "You still haven't explained what we must do to remove the curse from you."

The old woman stared at him for a long time, then shuddered. "That," she said, "will not be pretty."

CHAPTER 11

"BEWARE THE DANGLY-BOO!"

"At the edge of Bogfester Swamp is a tunnel. At the end of that tunnel is the Temple of Toadliness. Inside the temple lives the oldest toad of all."

"How old is he?" I asked without thinking.

"Uh-oh," said Urk, who was still sitting on my shoulder.

Without a word the old woman flicked her right hand at me. A string of green sparks flew in my direction, too fast for me to duck. They gathered on my lips, tingling like crazy. When I tried to open my mouth to shout, I found that my lips had been sealed shut!

"Didn't I tell you to be quiet?" snapped the old woman.

"Now, wait a minute," said Moongobble. "You can't just—"

"Silence, you old fool, or you're next! The boy was warned, wasn't he? And that gag won't hurt him. I could have done a lot worse if I had wanted. It would have been easier to take his head off—which would have kept him just as quiet. It took a lot of control for me to be that careful."

She must have seen the look of horror in my eyes, because she laughed and said, "Oh, don't be stupid, boy, I wouldn't really have done that. At least, I don't think I would have. Now, where was I? Oh, yes. The oldest toad—so old, in fact, that no one knows his age."

She looked directly at me when she said this, and I wondered if she had sealed my lips just because I had talked, or because I had made her mad by asking a question she didn't know the answer to.

"Anyway," she continued, "your job is to go to that toad and convince him to spit in a bottle."

"Spit in a bottle?" asked Moongobble, blinking a bit.

"What is this," screeched the old woman, "an echo chamber? Yes, spit in a bottle. That spit is the last thing I need to break the curse. Once you have it, bring it back to me."

"Spit in a bottle," muttered Urk. "Sheesh."

I noticed that he said it so quietly that the old woman couldn't hear him. I guess he didn't want to end up with his lips sealed shut too.

"Bogfester Swamp is very big," said Moongobble. "Can you tell us more about where to find this tunnel?"

"Do I have to do everything around here?" cried the old woman. She rolled her eyes, heaved a deep sigh, then said, "Oh, all right. Here."

Muttering a few words, she waved her hands. I heard a sizzling sound. A moment later a piece of paper fluttered out of the air.

Moongobble managed to grab it before it reached the floor.

"Ah," he said. "A very nice map! Thank you, madam."

"Take this, too," she said. "You'll need it."

She waved her hands again and a bottle fell out

of the air. Moongobble grabbed for it, but missed. I expected it to shatter on the stone floor of the cave, but Fireball swooped through Moongobble's legs. "Got it!" he cried, catching the bottle in his little red claws.

"What's it for?" asked Moongobble.

"The toad spit, of course," said the old woman. Rolling her eyes again, she muttered, "It really is impossible to get good help these days."

"Well, I guess we had better be going," said Moongobble.

"Not so fast. There's one more thing I must tell you. You may find many perils along the way. Most of them are marked on the map. But the greatest danger of all . . ."

She paused.

"Well, what?" cried Snelly. "What is it?"

I noticed that the old woman didn't seal *her* mouth shut, which didn't seem fair. Instead, she lowered her own voice and whispered, "Beware the Dangly-Boo." She closed her eyes and shook her head, as if even saying the name had been difficult. When she opened them again, she seemed surprised to see us. "Why are you still here? Go on! Get!"

But as we turned to go, she said, "No, wait just a moment. *He* stays here."

She was pointing to Oggledy Nork.

"You can't keep Oggledy!" cried Snelly.

"I most certainly can. He stays with me until you return. Sort of a . . . guarantee that you'll come back."

"Me stay with pretty lady," said Oggledy Nork, smiling.

"Well, I suppose if Oggledy doesn't object," said Moongobble, sounding uneasy. He turned to Oggledy Nork. "Are you sure it's all right?"

"Oggledy stay," he said, plunking down onto the floor so hard that he woke several bats. They went fluttering around above us.

"Well, all right," said Moongobble. He straightened his hat and said, "We're off to Bogfester Swamp!"

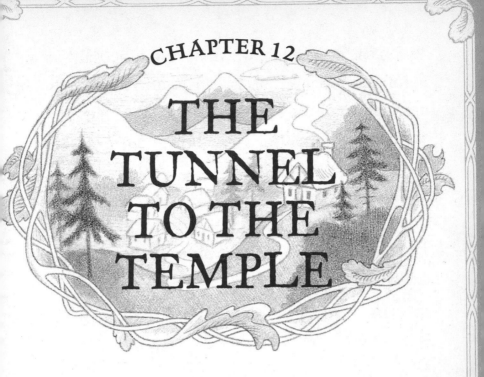

CHAPTER 12

THE TUNNEL TO THE TEMPLE

The seal on my lips wore off about an hour after we left the old woman's cave. My mouth was still tingling, but at least I could talk—and eat!

It took two days to reach Bogfester Swamp.

Actually, it's hard to tell exactly when you do reach Bogfester. The swamp doesn't have an edge, like a lake. Instead, the ground just gets squishier and squishier, and then somehow you realize you're in the swamp.

I guess it was official when Urk said, "Well, here we are."

The brown, murky water (we could actually smell it long before we got there) is dotted with small islands. Some of the islands are no bigger than a tabletop.

Insects buzzed around us.

A long-necked bird swooped low over the water.

Dead trees reached out with scraggly branches.

I was glad we didn't have to try to cross the swamp again.

"Which way now?" asked Snelly, her voice quieter than usual.

Moongobble studied the map. Urk was on his shoulder so he could look at it too. This was a good idea, since Moongobble had a habit of holding maps upside down.

"To the right," said Moongobble after a few minutes.

We began squishing in that direction. We tried to stay mostly on dry ground, but it wasn't easy. We cut walking sticks from some dead trees, and used them to check the ground ahead of us. Whenever we wanted to take a rest, we had to be careful the water didn't ooze up under our bottoms as we sat.

"How far is it to the tunnel?" whined Snelly the second time we took a break.

"Another half day's travel," replied Urk. "Assuming we don't sink in a mudhole along the way."

We didn't sink in a mudhole. On the other hand, when we reached the tunnel, I almost wished we had.

We didn't realize at first that it was the tunnel. That's because it looked more like a well, the kind that has a round stone wall around it. But when we got closer we saw a sign leaning against it:

TUNNEL TO THE TEMPLE OF TOADLINESS

~~GUESTS WELCOME~~

Only, *Guests Welcome* had been crossed out, and *Beware the Dangly-Boo* had been written underneath it.

"Well, that's encouraging," muttered Urk.

When we reached the stone circle and looked over the edge, we found a wooden ladder leaning against the inside wall. It stretched down until it disappeared into the darkness.

"Looks spooky," muttered Snelly.

"That shouldn't bother you," I said. "Heck, you live in Monster Mountain. Isn't that just as spooky?"

"It's home," replied Snelly with a sniff. "That's different."

"I'll go first," said Moongobble. He used the spell that makes his hat glow, then climbed over the stone wall and put his foot on the ladder. We heard a whirring sound. The rungs of the ladder started to move, carrying Moongobble swiftly away from us.

Leaning over the edge, I could see the glow of his hat. But the ladder was taking him down so fast that soon even the hat was out of view.

"Fireball!" I cried. "Fly down and make sure Moongobble is all right!"

The little dragon swooped into the well and plunged straight down. I put Urk on the stone wall. Snelly stood beside me. The three of us strained our eyes, trying to see into the darkness. Suddenly I spotted a spark of light. Fireball was coming back!

"Whew!" he gasped, as he came shooting up over the edge. "It's a *long* way down. But Moongobble is all right. He's waiting for you to join him."

"I'll go first," said Snelly, climbing onto the ladder.

"Why?" I asked.

"Because if you go first you can look up my dress!"

"That's disgusting!" I cried.

"Well, my momma says girls have to be careful about that kind of thing."

"All right, all right, feel free to go first," I said, waving her toward the well.

Snelly hopped onto the ladder. With a shout, she disappeared.

"Do you want to ride on my shoulder?" I asked Urk.

"I think that would be a good idea," he replied. "I'm not sure I could hold on to one of those rungs."

I put him on my shoulder, then climbed onto the ladder. Even though I knew what would happen, I yelped in surprise when the thing began to move. Soon it was going so fast, I felt my stomach pressing up against my throat.

Suddenly the ride got wilder as the ladder twisted and turned.

"Hold on, Edward!" cried Urk, scrambling down my neck and into my shirt.

"I'm trying!" I shouted back. "I'm trying!"

Down we went, and down, and down, until we stopped with a jolt. I saw a soft glow—Moongobble's hat.

"Whew," I said, climbing off the ladder. "That was some ride!"

"You're not kidding," said Snelly, who was still trying to straighten out her dress.

"Is everyone all right?" asked Moongobble.

"I'll let you know once I find my stomach," grumbled Urk. "I think I lost it about halfway down."

"Do we need to wait for it?" asked Moongobble, looking worried.

Urk sighed. "Don't be silly, Moongobble. I didn't really lose my stomach. It just felt like it."

Moongobble blinked, then said, "Oh, I see! All right, let's get going."

We had been walking for about five minutes when I saw some blue, slimy-looking stuff droop down from the tunnel's ceiling.

It was about to touch Snelly on the shoulder.

I rushed forward to warn her. But before I could say a thing, it shouted, "BOO!"

CHAPTER 13

EATING MAGIC

It was the loudest *BOO*! I had ever heard.

Snelly screamed.

At the same time, a huge chunk of blue goo fell from the tunnel ceiling onto her head.

It had to be the Dangly-Boo—what else would dangle from the ceiling and shout "Boo!" like that?

Moongobble hurried back to where Snelly stood. I was already at her side.

"Get it off!" shrieked Snelly. "Get it off, get it off, *get it off* !"

"Mmmmm," said the Dangly-Boo. "Nummy!"

"It's eating her head!" I cried.

"Am not!" yelled the Dangly-Boo. "Just eatin' the majik! It's nummy nummy nummy!"

I grabbed the blue thing and tried to pull it off Snelly's head. It felt like bread dough, only slimy. I pulled and pulled. It stretched and stretched. Suddenly the strand I was pulling on slipped out of my hand and snapped back to Snelly's head.

"Stand back, Edward!" cried Moongobble. "This calls for magic!"

"Uh-oh," said Urk.

Moongobble lifted his wand and shouted: "Iggledy Biggledy Skraypoff Dathing!"

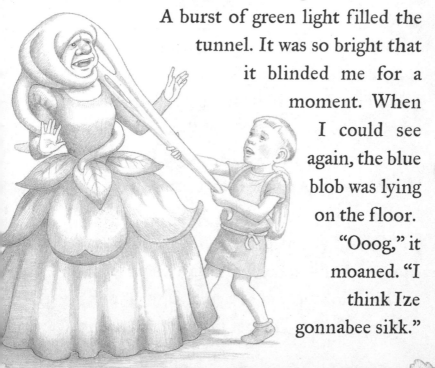

A burst of green light filled the tunnel. It was so bright that it blinded me for a moment. When I could see again, the blue blob was lying on the floor.

"Ooog," it moaned. "I think Ize gonnabee sikk."

"Serves you right," said Snelly.

I looked at her, then blinked in surprise. "Snelly, you've changed!"

She glared at me. "What do you mean?"

"It's like you've turned halfway back into your old self," said Urk.

"Did you do that?" she asked the Dangly-Boo.

"Uh-huh. I wuz eetin' the majik you wuz wearin'. It wuz yumzo."

"You were *eating* the magic?" asked Moongobble.

"Yeppers. Majik iz wut a Dangly-Boo eetz. It iz yumzo!"

"Ah," said Moongobble. "It must have eaten that spell I shot at it. That's why it let go of Snelly—it had all the magic it could hold!"

"Eat the rest of the spell!" cried Snelly. "I don't wanna be beautiful. I wanna be my old self again."

She ran over to the creature and tried to push her head into it.

"Ooog," groaned the Dangly-Boo. "Can't eetz no more now. I iz too full! Ize gonna puker!"

The blob turned away from us and made a disgusting sound. A blast of blue light shot out of what must have been its mouth. The light hit the far wall and began to drip down.

"Eeeuuwww!" cried Snelly. "That was gross!"

"Blurch," was all the Dangly-Boo could say.

Then it started to slide back up the closest wall. "Yew can goze on now," it moaned.

"But I want you to finish eating this spell!" whined Snelly.

The Dangly-Boo burped out a little burst of blue light. "Maybeez later," it groaned. Then it drooped down one long, blue, oozy tentacle and tapped Moongobble on the shoulder. "Yew needz to werk on yer majik. It tastez like old cheeze."

I could tell Moongobble was insulted. Looking cranky, he tucked his wand back into the belt of his robe and said, "Let's get going."

We continued down the tunnel.

I started to think about the fact that we were underneath Bogfester Swamp. I began to wonder what would happen if the tunnel gave way. We might be buried here!

Just when I was starting to get really frightened we saw a glow ahead of us.

We had reached the Temple of Toadliness!

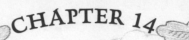

CHAPTER 14

THE TEMPLE OF TOADLINESS

"Wow," whispered Snelly as we stepped into the temple.

I might have said the same thing, except I was speechless.

The temple was a vast cavern, lit by soft orange light that filtered down from the ceiling. A stream cut across the middle of the cavern, flowing from one side to the other. A pretty little stone bridge led over the stream.

That was all interesting enough. But what took my breath away was what loomed at the far side of the stream: a statue of a toad that had to be at least fifty feet tall.

"Who dares enter the Temple of Toadliness?" boomed a voice.

It seemed to come from all around us.

"I am Moongobble the Magician," answered Moongobble, his own voice squeaking just a bit. "I have come with my companions in search of a cure to a curse."

"No one may enter this temple without the company of a toad," said the voice. It sounded displeased.

"We have a toad," bellowed Urk. "ME!"

"Ah. Then welcome. You may step forward."

We followed a path marked by round stones on either side. It led through the center of the cavern, right to the little bridge. As we crossed the bridge, a hole opened in the floor in front of the statue. A moment later a pillar rose from the opening. Perched on top of the pillar was a large toad, about twice the size of Urk. It was dressed in a white robe.

When we were about ten feet from the pillar, the toad pointed at us and said, "Stop right there."

We stopped.

After studying us for a few moments, the toad said, "Why have you come to the Temple of Toadliness?"

"We seek to right an ancient wrong," replied Moongobble.

"What wrong is this?"

"The Old Woman of the Forest of Night—"

"Her?" cried the toad. "You dare to speak to us of *her*? Not another word. That woman is no friend of the toads."

"Why not?" asked Moongobble.

"She is a breaker of vows!"

"What vow did she break?" asked Moongobble.

"She was supposed to marry our prince. Instead, she cursed him."

"But she cursed him because he was going to marry someone else instead," I blurted, forgetting that I should let Moongobble do the talking.

The toad glared at me. "The prince had ended that engagement. He was on the way to tell her this when she cast the curse of Oggledy Nork on him. It was by her own anger and impatience that she lost him, and doomed him and his children, and his children's children, and those still yet to come."

"That was long ago," said Moongobble. "It is time to bring the curse to an end. Now, if you'll just spit in this bottle—"

"Spit in a bottle?" boomed the toad. "YOU WANT ME TO SPIT IN A BOTTLE?"

He was so loud and angry that we all took a step back.

The toad began to swell with rage. His eyes were bulging dangerously. Just when I feared he might actually explode, the pillar he was standing on sank back into the floor.

We were alone in the Temple of Toadliness.

As least, I thought we were alone. Then, from somewhere above us, I heard the sound of stone rubbing against stone.

Looking up, I gasped in horror.

The giant toad statue had opened its eyes. With a grinding sound, it twisted its head to stare down at us.

Then it opened its mouth.

"Run!" cried Urk. "RUN!"

CHAPTER 15

TOAD CHASE

We turned and raced back across the cavern floor.

Fireball was flying ahead of us. He kept circling back, shouting, "Come on! Faster! *Faster*!"

As he swooped near my face, something thick and gray hissed past my shoulder. Just missing Fireball, it hit the floor with a huge cracking sound.

"Yikes!" shouted Fireball, shooting out a little burst of fire.

The thick gray thing disappeared. But not for long. A second later it zapped past me again. This time I realized what it was: the tongue of the giant statue!

Glancing over my shoulder, I saw the statue take a hop forward. It landed with such a thud that the entire cavern shook. Then its tongue shot out a third time.

"Fireball!" I cried. "Stop flying. *Stop flying*! It thinks you're a giant bug, and it's trying to catch you!"

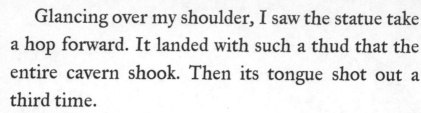

With a squawk, Fireball dropped to the cavern floor.

That stopped the stone toad's attempts to catch Fireball. That was the good news. The bad news was, now that the monster wasn't being distracted by Fireball, it decided to come after the rest of us instead. It hopped again, making another giant thud—this one so powerful that a crack split open in the cavern floor right ahead of us.

"Jump!" cried Moongobble.

I was a little worried about Moongobble, but he made it over the gap in the floor with no problem. To my astonishment, it was Snelly who fell in.

"Help!" she wailed. "HEEEEELP!"

I turned back and stuck out my hand. She grabbed it, and I pulled her up.

THWOCK! The toad's tongue zapped down beside us.

"Get moving!" bellowed Urk, who was riding on Moongobble's shoulder.

"It's this stupid new body," grumbled Snelly. "I don't know how to use it."

She stumbled again, but managed not to fall. As I helped her to her feet, I noticed Fireball dragging himself along the floor ahead of us. "I hate crawling," he muttered. "I just hate it!"

THWOCK!

The giant gray tongue hit the floor about two feet behind him. It was too much for the little dragon; he took to the air again.

"Faster!" cried Moongobble. "Faster!"

THWOCK! *THWOCK*!

Just as we reached the little bridge, the toad made another leap forward. The bridge trembled under our feet. Then the toad's tongue hit the end of it. With a shudder, the back part of the bridge collapsed.

We skidded down the front side and hurtled onward.

THU-DOOM! *THU-DOOM*! *THU-DOOM*!

That was the sound of the giant stone toad hopping toward us. I was terrified that it was going to crack not only the floor, but also the roof. Soon, all of Bogfester Swamp might come flooding into the cavern.

"We're almost there!" cried Snelly. But just as we reached the tunnel where we had entered the cavern, the toad's tongue shot past us again. It struck right above the opening that would let us out. With a nasty rumble, a cascade of broken rock fell over the exit, blocking it completely.

We were trapped in the cavern, and the giant toad was almost on us.

CHAPTER 16

DANGLY-BARF

We pressed ourselves against the wall, waiting for the end.

"We're all gonna die," moaned Snelly.

The mice in Moongobble's hat were shrieking.

"Death by toad," muttered Urk. "I never thought *that* would be the way I went."

Moongobble raised his wand and cried, "Iggledy, Biggledy, Stoppa Datode!"

A burst of light shot from the end of his wand. It struck the statue right between the eyes.

To my surprise, the toad actually stopped.

It crossed its enormous eyes, looking puzzled.

Then it burped.

A horrible smell—the smell of old, amazingly stinky cheese—washed over us. It was like being caught in a fartstorm.

The toad covered its mouth, looking embarrassed.

"I don't think that's going to be enough, Moongobble," said Urk.

He was right. The toad was about to take another hop toward us. I pressed myself to the wall, wishing I could say good-bye to Mother and Father. Suddenly I heard a voice from *behind* me. Just in time, I realized what it was.

"Get out of the way!" I screamed, diving to my right.

Fireball shot straight up. Moongobble, Urk, and Snelly dashed to the left as a burst of sickly green light blew open the blocked tunnel. Chunks of stone went flying in all directions. The green light began spreading across the floor in a disgusting puddle.

"Ooog," said a familiar voice. "I think I iz puked out now. Feelz much gooder. Yew gott zum moor majik I canz eet?"

Urk hopped over to the hole. "Out of the way!" he bellowed. "We're coming through!"

He disappeared into the opening. Snelly scrambled after him, followed quickly by Fireball. Moongobble and I plunged into the hole at the same time—and got stuck!

As we struggled to free ourselves, the giant toad made its next hop. The wall quivered with the force of his landing. Any second I knew I might feel that huge tongue smack my butt and pull me back into the toad's mouth.

"Good-bye, Moongobble," I said.

"Good-bye, Edward. I'm sorry I got you into this mess."

But before the toad could get us, the Dangly-Boo wrapped a pair of tentacles around our arms and yanked us forward. We landed with a *thud* on the tunnel floor.

I tried to gasp out a thank you, but stopped when five feet of giant stone tongue shot through the spot the Dangly-Boo had barfed open.

"Let's get outta here!" cried Snelly.

I didn't need the next shake of the tunnel to

convince me she was right. We began to run again. After about a hundred feet we stopped, gasping for breath, but safe.

"Thank you," said Moongobble, making a bow to the Dangly-Boo.

"Wuz akzident," it said, sounding almost shy. Turning to Snelly it added, "Can eetz more majik now? Pleeze?"

"You bet!" cried Snelly. She bent down and reached for the creature. It squished in the middle, then stretched up a pair of long, blobby arms to grab her by the ears. Once it had a good hold, it pulled itself up and wrapped itself around her head, covering her face entirely.

"She won't be able to breathe!" I cried.

"Shut up!" shouted Snelly, her voice muffled by the Dangly-Boo. "I can breathe just fine."

"Yumzo," said the Dangly-Boo happily. "I iz feeling much gooder now."

"I'm glad one of us is feeling better," Urk said, "since the rest of us have failed completely."

Moongobble's shoulders slumped. "I guess I'm not as good a magician as I had hoped." He sighed heavily, then said, "Well, let's head back to the old woman's cave. We'll tell her we failed, and take Oggledy Nork home with us."

I had never heard him sound so sad. He began to trudge down the tunnel.

CHAPTER 17

I LOSE MY TEMPER

Except for occasional sounds of, "Yum-yum-yumzo!" from the Dangly-Boo, our trip back to the old woman's cave was quieter than usual. This was because none of us felt like talking. We had failed, and it looked as if Oggledy Nork would have to bear his curse forever.

The only one who was happy was Snelly, who kept getting shorter and uglier as the Dangly-Boo ate the spell that had made her tall and beautiful. By the time we stopped to rest on the first night, she was her old self again.

"Boy, that's a relief!" she cried as the Dangly-Boo let go of her head and plopped to the ground.

The Dangly-Boo itself just lay on its back—at least, I think it was on its back—moaning, "Oooog. Gud mealie!"

Though bringing the Dangly-Boo along had solved Snelly's problem of turning back to herself, the next morning we realized it had provided us with a new problem. This was because the Dangly-Boo couldn't walk. The reason was simple: It didn't have anything to walk with! Oh, it could stick out parts of itself to grab onto a cave wall and pull itself up. It could slide along smooth stone. But the forest floor was not made for sliding on, and the creature wasn't solid enough to put out any kind of "leg" that would support it. Every time it tried to stand up, its "legs" would wobble for a minute. Then it would cry, "Whoopsie!" and fall back to the ground.

"I can't carry the thing," fretted Moongobble. "It will eat my magic!"

Fireball and Urk couldn't carry the Dangly-Boo either—they just weren't built for it. So it ended up being my job. We took everything out of my pack (we had eaten most of the food we were carrying, so it was almost empty, anyway) and stuffed the Dangly-Boo inside. I was afraid it might resent this, but it said happily, "Gud! Iz nize an dark here! Canz uze a nap!"

Late that afternoon we reached the old woman's cave. As usual, Fireball talked our way past the snakes that hung over the entrance. When we entered, I heard a strange sound: two voices—one old and creaky, the other low and gruff—chanting, "Patty-cake, patty-cake, baker's man! Bake me a cake as quick as you can!"

Moongobble and I looked at each other in puzzlement, then hurried forward. What we saw matched what we had heard—the old woman and Oggledy Nork were playing patty-cake!

"Oh!" cried the old woman when we came in.

She sounded embarrassed.

"Were you playing patty-cake?" asked Snelly.

"Don't be stupid!" snapped the old woman. "Of course we weren't. Besides, I had to do something to keep Oggledy Nork calm."

Which seemed to me to mean they *had* been playing patty-cake.

Before I could figure out what that might mean, Oggledy Nork bellowed, "Calm! Susan keep Oggledy Nork calm!"

"Susan?" I asked, blinking in surprise.

"Shut up!" shouted the old woman. Turning to Oggledy Nork, she said, "And you be quiet too, you naughty boy." But she patted his cheek when she said it, and her voice was so sweet it was kind of sickening. Turning to the rest of us, she said, "What are you doing here?"

"We have returned to take Oggledy Nork home with us," said Moongobble.

"Don't wanna go!" said Oggledy Nork, plunking down on the floor.

"Oh, you wicked boy," giggled the old woman.

"Oggledy!" cried Snelly, "you have to come!"

Oggledy Nork shook his head stubbornly. "Oggledy Nork stay here. Oggledy Nork like it here!"

"Are you sure?" asked Moongobble.

Oggledy Nork nodded. "Me like it here. Me like the cave. Me like the snakes. Me like the Susan!"

I wasn't sure, but I thought I saw the old woman blush. "Naughty boy," she murmured again, smacking his hand lightly. Turning to Moongobble, her face darkened and she demanded, "Why have you come back for him? Did you give up?"

Moongobble shook his head. "Of course we did not give up. We tried our best at the Temple of Toadliness, but failed."

Her eyes widened in astonishment. "You went there and *survived*?" Then she added quickly, "I mean, um, so you didn't get the bottle of spit?"

All of a sudden I understood. The old woman had never expected us to come back. "It was a trick, wasn't it?" I cried.

"What do you mean?" she asked.

"I mean you *never* thought we would make it back with that toad spit. You knew that the minute we asked the old toad priest to spit in a bottle, he would get so mad that terrible things would happen. You thought we would die there!"

She put her hand to her chest and tried to look innocent.

And that was when I lost my temper. I had had enough of this person. Even though I knew it wasn't smart, I cried, "You are a horrible, evil old woman. Why do you do these things?"

Her look of innocence vanished. Eyes blazing, she cried, "Who are you to ask me such a question?"

"I'm the boy whose father you turned into the Weeping Werewolf, that's who! Who are you that you think you have a right to be so mean?"

"Who am I?" she shrieked. "I am the woman whose heart was broken and whose life was stolen! I am the woman who lives alone. I am the woman who has no choice! I am the Old Woman of the Forest of Night—and I have had just about enough of *you*!"

She raised her hands to cast a spell.

"Wait!" bellowed Oggledy Nork.

He grabbed the old woman's hands. She pulled them free, but Oggledy Nork had given me just enough time. Snatching the Dangly-Boo from my pack, I threw it right at her.

CHAPTER 18

THE LETTER THAT CAME LATE

The Dangly-Boo wrapped itself around the old woman's head.

She began to scream.

"Hey, you . . . you *thing*!" cried Oggledy Nork. "Let go of the Susan!"

He started to pry at the Dangly-Boo. But it clung tight, chortling, "Yumzo Yumzo Yumzo! Gud majik! Spicy! Well-aged! Hintz of melon and guano! Iz best majik I ever eetzed!"

A minute later Oggledy Nork finally managed to pull a bit of the Dangly-Boo loose. He started backward, stretching the creature so far I was afraid it would break in half.

"Yumzo!" it cried one last time. Then it let go of the old woman, snapping into Oggledy Nork's big hands.

To my surprise, the old woman didn't look any the worse for the wear. In fact, except for the unexpected smile on her face, she didn't look any different at all.

"You did it!" she cried. "You removed the curse!"

"Wuz yumzo!" said the Dangly-Boo happily. "Thankz!"

Then it burped out a burst of pink and yellow light.

"If we removed the curse, that means you have to remove the curse from Oggledy Nork," said Urk quietly.

The old woman frowned. "I know I promised. And I'm feeling quite a bit . . . different. I don't really want to be mean about this, but the truth is, I kind of like him the way he is."

"But I'm not the way I was," said a new voice.

I turned and gasped. Oggledy Nork had changed

into something I can only call a Half-Oggledy. He was tall, but not as tall as he had been. He also looked quite a bit older—not as old as the old woman, but older than he had been.

I could even see a resemblance to his brother, the Rusty Knight.

His outfit hung loosely on him. Reaching into it, he pulled out a piece of paper. "You should read this," he said.

The old woman took it from him.

"What does it say?" demanded Snelly.

The old woman shook her head. "My eyes are too old. The light is too dim. I can't read it."

But I thought she must have read at least part of it, because I saw tears in her eyes.

"That's all right, Susan," said Half-Oggledy. "I know it by heart. It's from my ancestor."

Clearing his throat, he began to recite the letter:

My Dearest Toadlietta,

I have not told you all you need to know.

In my human life, I am the oldest son of a wealthy man. He long ago arranged for me to marry a woman from a nearby family, also wealthy. She is sweet and lovely, but she is not you. She is fair and fine, but she is not you. She has hair like silk and skin like satin, but she does not understand the swamp or the moon, or the way a fly tastes on the tongue when you have just snatched it from the air. She is not you, and I have decided I would rather be a toad with you one day a month than a lord in her castle for all the other days of my life.

We were to be wed tomorrow. I am going now to tell her of my choice. I am writing this letter in case anything happens to me before I can return to tell you this myself, in my toad shape.

With all my toadly heart,

Bufemus Nork

Staring at Half-Oggledy, the old woman said, "Where did you get this?"

He smiled. "It is the Nork family treasure. It has been passed from father to son for many years. Each of us has been told that if we ever had a chance, we must deliver it to the Old Woman of the Forest of Night. I am sorry I did not give it to you sooner, but when I was Oggledy Nork, I did not have enough sense to do so."

Crumpling the letter against her chest, the old woman burst into sobs, then turned and ran into the back of the cave.

Half-Oggledy ran after her.

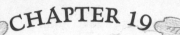

CHAPTER 19

MORE PEOPLE TO LOVE

"I still don't understand," said my mother.

It was a week later. Moongobble and Urk had come to dinner at our cottage, and Mother and Father were asking them about our adventures.

"What don't you understand?" I asked.

"Well, first of all, why did Oggledy Nork only turn halfway back to himself?"

"I have a guess about that," said Moongobble.

"Which is?" asked Father.

"I think that when Edward used the Dangly-Boo to take the curse off the old woman, half of the Oggledy curse disappeared too."

"Why would that happen?" asked Mother.

"Rules of magic," said Urk, who was sitting on Moongobble's shoulder. "Because she had promised to remove the Oggledy curse, we think that once we took the curse off her, half of the other curse went away by itself."

"It happened automagically," said Moongobble, nodding his head.

"She would have to work to take it away completely," continued Urk. "But the fact that we had met her condition meant that half the spell was broken instantly."

"And a good thing it was," said Moongobble. "Otherwise Oggledy Nork wouldn't have remembered that letter."

"I can't believe how different she is now," said my father, shaking his head.

The reason Father knew what the old woman was like now was that she and Half-Oggledy had come back to Pigbone with us. They were going to get married! Right now they were staying in the Rusty Knight's old house, but they planned to build a house of their own soon. Snelly had stayed with them for a few days, until she decided she had better go back to Monster Mountain before her mother got angry with her.

"What about the Rusty Knight?" continued my mother. "What happened to him?"

Moongobble shook his head. "I truly don't know. Next week Edward and I should probably make a trip to Fortress Nork to check on him."

As it turned out, something happened the next day that made the trip unnecessary. I was at Moongobble's cottage, talking to the Dangly-Boo. The creature was living on a dead tree we had brought inside for him to dangle from. Moongobble was feeding it a new spell every day. After it ate the spell, the Dangly-Boo would make suggestions about how to improve the magic. It was just explaining to me what that day's spell tasted like when we heard a loud knocking at the door.

"Companee!" said the Dangly-Boo happily. "Dangly-Booz luv companee! Gotz awful lonelee in that tunnl."

When I opened the door I saw a tall, hairy man.

He looked like Half-Oggledy, but not exactly.

"Who are you?" I asked.

"Don't you recognize me, Edward?"

Urk came hopping to the door. He began to laugh. "Well, *I* know who you are."

And then I knew too. "Rusty Knight?" I asked in amazement.

He smiled. "That's what folks here used to call me. I'm not sure it fits anymore. I just got back from Fortress Nork. I wanted to say hello, and thank you and Moongobble and Urk for helping to lift the family curse. Or, at least, half-lifting it." His smile grew broader. "The fact is, halfway is just fine. I rather like my new self."

"Greetings, friend," said Moongobble, who had joined us at the door. "What are you going to do now?"

"Why, I've come back to live in Pigbone! This is my home, much more than Fortress Nork. Especially now that my brother is here too."

I can't quite figure out if we have three new neighbors, or just two. After all, the Rusty Knight has lived here from before the time I was born. But the man who lives in his house now is not the Rusty Knight we used to know. He's someone different.

"I'm not sure I like all these changes," I said to Mother that night, when I had come back from Moongobble's cottage.

She smiled. "You're changing too, Edward. You're a much bigger boy now than you were when Moongobble first came to town. Too big, do you think, to sit in your mother's lap?"

I shook my head and smiled. Mother was sitting in the rocking chair that Father had made for her while I was off on our adventure. I climbed into her lap.

She put her arms around me.

"What will it be like when the baby comes?" I asked, resting my head against her.

"Different," she said, stroking my hair. "But different isn't always bad, son. It was different when you brought your father home after he had been missing all those years. But that wasn't bad, was it?"

"Of course not!"

"Right," said Mother softly. "It was just one more person to love. And that's what it will be like when the baby comes."

"What about the Rusty Knight and his brother and the old woman?"

"Just more people to love, Edward. Just more people to love."

Like what you've read?
Turn the page for an excerpt
from Bruce Coville's
Goblins in the Castle,
available now!

Discovery in the Dungeon

I was found on the drawbridge of Toad-in-a-Cage Castle on a cold December night. I was naked, they tell me, wrapped only in a blanket and tucked in a basket. If the Baron had not been out riding that night he would not have seen me, and I would have been buried beneath the snow by morning.

To the surprise of Hulda, his housekeeper, the Baron didn't send me away. Instead, he hired a nurse to come and take care of me.

I liked Nurse, despite her unusual fondness for toads. However when I was about five she fell into the moat and was eaten by something or other.

After that I pretty much took care of myself.

I had the run of the castle and could go anywhere I wanted—except the North Tower, which was always locked. Naturally, I wanted to know what was up there. But I learned early on not to ask about it. Questions upset people.

Not that there were many people to upset; only the Baron, Hulda, and Karl, the young man who tended the library.

I liked Karl. He was very smart, and when he had time he would give me lessons. However, this did not happen often, because caring for the library was a big job. (The Baron owned so many books he had had to knock out the walls between seven rooms to hold them all!)

Most of what I knew about the outside world came from the books Karl shared with me.

The library itself was my favorite place in the castle. Its floor was covered by a thick, soft carpet, its walls made of dark wood. Mazes of tall, book-crammed shelves filled the interior. The windows, which curved out from the side of the building, were twice as tall as a man; the huge velvet curtains that covered them used to be red and were still soft and warm. On cold days I liked to take a book and curl up on one of the sills. Wrapping a curtain around me like a blanket, I would alternate between reading and staring out at the distant village, the forest, the mountains.

I often wondered what it was like out there, beyond the castle walls that I had never left.

From one of the windows I could see the North

Tower, which was shrouded in mist on even the sunniest of days.

One rainy evening in October Karl was repairing books, Hulda was sleeping, and the Baron was hidden away with one of the mysterious visitors that sometimes came to the castle gate. I was on my own, as usual. For some reason—perhaps because the voices that moaned along the hallway outside my room had been so loud the night before—I couldn't settle down to read.

I went to my room and played with Mervyn, the rat I had tamed the year before. When he ran off, I decided to go to bed. Slipping out of my clothes, I pulled on my nightshirt, then drew aside the curtain surrounding my bed and climbed beneath the covers.

I couldn't sleep.

A streak of lightning sizzled through the night. I liked to watch lightning, so I got up and sat by my window. But the lightning did not continue. After a while I grew tired of watching the thick drops splat against the glass and decided to go exploring. I had been exploring the castle for years and still hadn't discovered everything about it—partly because it was so huge, partly because it had so many secret passages and hidden rooms. These were what I looked for when I explored. To find them I pushed bricks, moved picture frames, and fiddled with the knobs carved in the mantelpieces of the fireplaces.

Lighting a candle, I went to my own fireplace, which was tall enough to stand in. I pushed a certain brick and the fireplace swung around, putting me in the passage behind it.

I had discovered this passage when I was only six. Once in it, I could get into any other room on my floor. But since it *was* my floor, since I was the only person living there, it didn't do me much good.

The worst thing about the secret passages was that they were so dark. When I first started exploring I had tried taking torches with me, but somehow the Baron always found out and told me not to. I understood why; some passages were lined with wood, or even drapes, and it would have been easy to start a fire in them. Finally I had started carrying candles. They didn't provide *much* light, but they were better than nothing, and the Baron never said anything about them.

About a hundred feet from my room a hidden stairway led to some secret rooms in the East Tower. Holding my candle before me, I made my way to the steps, then climbed three flights to a room dominated by a clock several feet taller than I am. I had seen this clock many times without ever really looking at it. But on this day I felt a hunch about it.

Opening the glass-paneled door, I put my hand inside. The wood behind the counterweights seemed solid. But when I climbed a chair and moved the hands of the clock to point straight up, as if it were midnight, I heard the familiar whisper of a sliding panel. The back of the clock had disappeared!

I jumped off the chair. Squeezing my way through the clock's door, I found myself in a narrow passage. Keeping one hand against the smooth, cool stones of the wall, I moved slowly forward. Even with the candle, I didn't notice the stairway going down until I put my foot on a spot that wasn't there.

The jolt knocked the breath out of me. Had I not been going slowly, I probably would have broken my neck falling down that stairwell, which stretched as far as I could see, no matter how high I lifted the candle.

I began to count as I walked. Fifty steps. A hundred steps. Two hundred steps. By now I must be down among the wine cellars.

Three hundred steps! I began to wish I had changed back into my clothes. The air was cool down here.

I had to be far past the wine cellars now, all the way to the dungeons. I shivered. I had never been to the dungeons before. In

fact, I only knew they existed because Karl had told me about them, hinting that they held dark secrets.

Four hundred steps. Four hundred and fifty.

How far into the earth does this stairway go? I wondered as I neared the five hundredth step. But number five hundred was the end of it.

Keeping my left hand pressed against the wall, I moved slowly forward.

Fifteen paces brought me to a wooden door held together by thick iron crosspieces.

I could either turn back or open the door. Grasping the latch, which was enormous, I struggled to lift it without making any sound. It's hard to say why I felt a need to move so quietly. I was sure I was alone. But something about moving in the darkness inspires silence.

Besides, I liked to keep secrets.

When I managed to lift the latch the door swung open easily.

I saw a light flickering in the distance.

My heart began to beat more rapidly. *Who could possibly be down here?*

Again I thought about turning back. But my curiosity was driving me on, and I felt confident I could move so silently no one would know I was coming—though I don't think even then I really believed there was anyone there.

I started toward the light. Soon I could tell that it came from beyond a curve in the wall. As I continued forward I could see the outlines of the stones in the floor. The wall itself was damp and slightly chill beneath my fingers. Even so, I pressed myself against it when I reached the curve. Inching my way forward, I saw the source of the light—a torch, stuck in a bracket.

To my astonishment, I also heard someone singing! The voice was little more than a low growl, but the tune was rollicking.

I could not make out the words.

I stopped and tried to talk myself into turning back. But in my whole life I had never met anyone besides Nurse, the Baron, Hulda, and Karl. I had to know who was down here.

Dropping to the floor, I set my candle down and began to creep forward. Beyond the torch an open door led to the source of the singing.

Closer I crept, closer still, until I had almost reached the door. I took a deep breath.

Slowly, ever so slowly, I poked my head around the corner.

Igor

"BOO!"

I screamed and jumped into the air, then landed on the floor with a thump. My heart was pounding so hard I thought it would beat its way out of my chest, my hands trembling so violently I could not push myself off the floor.

About three feet away from me a strange-looking person rolled on the floor, shaking with laughter. His snorts echoed weirdly from the stone walls.

After a while the man (if man he was) caught his breath and pushed himself to a sitting position. He had huge, deep-set eyes and a balding head that glowed softly in the torchlight. His nose looked as if it had once been squashed, for it spread broadly across his face—most of which was covered by a huge black beard that hung halfway to his knees. A large hump rose from the upper right side of his back. He wore an old fur coat that reached almost to his feet, which were covered by battered boots laced with thick strips of leather.

Next to him lay a lumpy brown something.

Still chuckling, he pointed at me and said, "Good joke on you, boy!" His voice was low and gravelly.

I pushed myself to my knees. "Who are you?" I asked. "What are you doing here?"

The stranger stopped snorting. "Me Igor. *Igor!* Igor live here. Igor always live here."

"What do you mean 'always'? I've lived here for eleven years, and I've never seen you."

He smiled, displaying a set of crooked yellow teeth. "You are baby in this castle. Igor been here more than . . ." He stopped and began to count on his fingers. Finally he looked up and said, "More than six hundred years."

It was my turn to snort. "No one has lived anywhere for six hundred years. People die before they get that old."

Igor shrugged, causing his hump to shift like someone rolling under a blanket. "Igor done that before. Not much fun." Grabbing one of the thick, rusty chains that hung from the wall, he pulled himself to his feet. The hump caused him to stoop, so he was only a little taller than me.

Reaching down, he picked up the brown something that had been lying beside him.

"What's that?" I asked, climbing to my feet as well.

"Igor's *bear!*" he replied, swinging it through the air and whacking me on the head.

"Hey!" I yelled, expecting it to hurt. It didn't. Whatever this bear was, it was soft.

"See?" said Igor proudly. "Bear good for bopping."

"Can I look at it?" I asked, holding out my hands.

Igor stared at me. "No bopping!" he warned.

I shook my head. "No bopping," I promised, not bothering to add that I would have been terrified of trying to bop him.

Igor handed me the bear. I had never seen anything like it. Between two and three feet high, it was made of fur sewn together with crude stitches and stuffed with something soft. It was like a doll, only shaped like a bear instead of a human.

"Where did you get this?"

"Made it," said Igor, reaching out to take it back. I let go reluctantly. The bear was nice to hold.

Tucking the bear under his arm, Igor moved a few steps away. His left boot was twisted sideways, and it dragged behind him, giving him an odd, shuffling gait.

"How did you get here?" I asked.

"Igor always been here," he said with another of those shrugs. "This Igor's home."

"Surely you weren't born here."

"Born?" Igor wrinkled his brow as if he didn't understand. Then he smiled. "Oh, *born*. No, Igor not born here. Don't think Igor was born. Igor just *is*. Igor just *here*."

Clearly I wasn't going to get anywhere with this line of questioning. "Where do you get your food?" I asked.

"Take it."

I don't know what prompted me to get indignant

about that, but I did. "I think I had better tell the Baron about you," I said. "You live in his castle without his knowing. You steal his food. He's not going to like this."

I regretted the remark the moment I made it. For one thing, the Baron could spare the food. For another, Igor swung to face me with a look that made me want to melt into the stones of the floor.

"Stupid boy!" he cried, shaking his bear at me. "You not tell Baron. Not tell anyone—or Igor fix you good."

I shivered.

"Igor got to eat," he continued in a voice like a growl. "Igor got to live. Igor live here. Only food in dungeon is mushrooms and little critters. Igor need more than that, so Igor take food. *That part of the deal!*"

"What deal?"

"Igor got job. Igor do job, Igor get food."

"What is your job?"

"Igor watch things."

"What things?"

He put a crooked finger to his lips and shook his head. "Old Baron say, 'Igor, if you know what good for you, keep your mouth shut.' Igor know what good for Igor. Igor keep mouth shut. Boy keep mouth shut, too, if boy know what good for *him*."

"My name William . . . *is* William," I said, inching my way toward the door. "And I won't tell anyone about you. I promise."

"Wait," said Igor. "Don't go. Stay and talk to Igor."

He put his face close to mine and grinned. "Igor like talking to William."

Though he scared me, I liked talking to Igor, too. I had almost convinced myself to stay when he got an odd look on his face. Furrowing his brow, he whispered, "William hear that?"

I listened and felt a chill. Something was moving in the darkness beyond Igor's cell.

"Go, William!" he cried. "Go now! Run fast. Come back later."

"Wait," I said. "What's going on? Will you be all right?"

"Go!" cried Igor. "This Igor's job. William go! Now!"

Without waiting to see if I had done as he commanded he went shuffling down the corridor, dragging his bear by a back leg.

Soon he had disappeared in the darkness.